Clementine

Clementine

SARA PENNYPACKER

PICTURES BY
Marla Frazee

𝒟ℐ𝒮𝒩ℰ𝒴 • HYPERION
Los Angeles   New York

All rights reserved. Published by Disney • Hyperion, an imprint of Disney Book Group.

For information address Disney • Hyperion, 125 West End Avenue, New York, New York 10023-6387.

First hardcover edition, September, 2006.
First paperback edition, February, 2008.
30 29 28 27 26 25
FAC-026988-19263
This book is set in Fournier.
Designed by Michael Farmer
Printed in the United States of America
Library of Congress Control Number for the hardcover edition: 2005050458
ISBN-13: 978-0-7868-3883-7
ISBN-10: 0-7868-3883-3
Visit www.disneybooks.com

SUSTAINABLE FORESTRY INITIATIVE Certified Sourcing
www.sfiprogram.org
SFI-00993

THIS LABEL APPLIES TO TEXT STOCK

Many thanks to Kate Herrill for her drawings on pages 10, 42, 94, and 112.

For Bill, Clementine's
father in every way
——S.P.

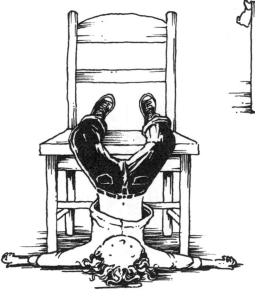

To my big brother,
Mark Frazee, who
thinks I'm an idiot
——M.F.

I have had not so good of a week.

Well, Monday was a pretty good day, if you don't count Hamburger Surprise at lunch and Margaret's mother coming to get her. Or the stuff that happened in the principal's office when I got sent there to explain that Margaret's hair was not my fault and besides she looks okay without it, but I couldn't because Principal Rice was gone, trying to calm down Margaret's mother.

Someone should tell you not to answer the phone in the principal's office, if that's a rule.

Okay, fine, Monday was not so good of a day.

Which was a surprise, because it started off with two lucky signs, which fooled me. First, there were exactly enough banana slices in my cereal: one for every spoonful. Then, as soon as I got to school, my teacher said, "The following students are excused from journal writing so they can go to the art room to work on their 'Welcome to the Future' projects." And I was one of the following students!

So instead of having to think up things to write in my journal, which I hate, I got to glue and paint stuff, which I love.

Margaret was in the art room, too. When I sat down next to her, she threw herself across the Princess-from-the-Future mask she was gluing sparkles onto. "Remember the rules," she warned.

Margaret is in fourth grade and I am in third. She thinks that that makes her the boss of me. I hate Margaret's rules.

"You can't touch my stuff," she said. Which she always says.

"Why?" I said. Which *I* always say.

"Because it's the rule," Margaret said. Which she always says.

"Why?" I said.

"Because you can't touch my stuff," she said.

And then I pointed out the window. Which wasn't exactly lying, because I didn't say there was something out there.

While Margaret was looking out the window, I accidentally touched her mask.

Twice. Okay, fine.

Then I got busy working on my project so I wouldn't have to hear any "Clementine-pay-attention!"s.

Except I did anyway. Which was unfair because each time, I was the *only* person in the whole art room who *was* paying attention. Which is why I could tell everyone right in the middle of the Pledge of Allegiance that the lunchroom lady was sitting in the janitor's car and they were kissing. *Again.* No one else saw this disgusting scene, because no one else was paying attention out the window!

And after that, when it was my turn to pass around the stapler, I could tell everyone that the art teacher's scarf had an egg stain on it that looked—if you squinted—exactly like a pelican, which nobody else had noticed.

"Clementine, you need to pay attention!" the art teacher said one more time. And just like the other times, I *was* paying attention.

I was paying attention to Margaret's empty seat.

Margaret had been excused to go to the girls' room, and when she left she had scrunched-up don't-cry eyes and a pressed-down don't-cry mouth. And she had been gone a really long time, even for Margaret, who washes her hands one finger at a time.

"I need to go to the girls' room," I told my teacher.

And that's where Margaret was, all right: curled up under the sink with her head on her knees.

"Margaret!" I gasped. "You're sitting on the floor!"

Margaret hitched herself over to the side a little so I could see: she'd placed a germ-protective layer of paper towels under her.

"Still," I said. "What's the matter?"

Margaret pressed her head down harder into her knees, which were all shiny with tears. She pointed up. Lying on the sink, next to a pair of Do-Not-Remove-from-the-Art-Room scissors, was a chunk of straight brown hair.

Uh-oh.

"Come out, Margaret," I said. "Let me see."

Margaret shook her head. "I'm not coming out until it's grown back."

"Well, I think I see a germ crawling up your dress."

Margaret jumped out from under the sink.

She looked at herself in the mirror and began to cry again. "I got glue in my hair," she sobbed. "I was just trying to cut it out. . . ."

Margaret's hair was halfway-down-her-back long. It was hard not to notice that the whole part over her left ear was missing.

"Maybe if we evened up a chunk over your right ear . . ." I suggested.

Margaret wiped her eyes dry and nodded. She handed me the scissors.

I cut. We looked back in the mirror.

"It's like bangs." I tried to cheer her up. "Sort of."

"Except bangs are in your front hair, not the sides," Margaret reminded me. Then she took a deep sigh, picked up the scissors, and cut off all the hair over her forehead.

Now the front half of her hair was all chopped off and the back half was long and straight and shiny.

"Not so good," Margaret said, looking in the mirror.

"Not so good," I agreed.

We looked at her not-so-good hair in the mirror

for a really, really long time without saying anything, which is very hard for me. Then Margaret's
bottom lip began to shiver and her eyes filled up
with tear-balls again. She handed the scissors back
to me, and then she closed her eyes and turned
around.

"All of it?" I asked.

"All of it."

So I did. Which is not exactly easy with those
plastic art scissors, let me tell you. And just as I
was finishing, the art teacher came in looking
for us.

"Clementine!" she shouted. *"What are you
doing?"*

And then Margaret went all historical, and the
art teacher went all historical, and nobody could
think of anything to do except the regular thing,
which is: send *me* to the principal's office.

While I was waiting there, I drew a picture of Margaret with her chopped-off hair. I made her look beautiful, like a dandelion. Here is a picture of that:

If they had a special class for gifted kids in art, I would definitely be in it. But they don't, which is also unfair—only for math and English. I am not so good at English, okay, fine. But this year I am in the gifted class for math. And here is the bad surprise—so far, no gifts.

I told Principal Rice about that problem when she got back from calming down Margaret's mother.

"So far, no gifts," I told her, extremely politely.

Principal Rice rolled her eyes to the ceiling then, like she was looking for something up there. Ceiling snakes maybe, just waiting to drip on you. That's what I used to be afraid of when I was little, anyway. Now I am not afraid of anything.

Okay, fine, I am afraid of pointy things. But that is all. And boomerangs.

"Clementine, you need to pay attention," said Principal Rice. "We need to discuss Margaret's hair. What are you doing on the floor?"

"Helping you look for ceiling snakes," I reminded her.

"*Ceiling* snakes? *What* ceiling snakes?" she asked.

See what I mean? Me—paying attention; every-

body else—not. I am amazed they let someone with this problem be the boss of a school.

"All right, now, Clementine," Principal Rice said in her I'm-trying-to-be-patient-but-it's-getting-harder voice. "Why did you cut off Margaret's hair?"

"I was helping," I said.

And then I told Principal Rice about how I'd helped her, too. "I answered the phone while you were gone. I ordered some new school pets, and I told the gym teacher we are never going to play dodgeball again, and I made two appointments for you. The phone kept going dead, so I guess it's busted. But at least I helped you a little."

That's what *I* thought.

There is a look they teach a person to make in principal school that is not very nice.

Margaret was waiting for me in the lobby of our apartment building when I got off the bus after school. I showed her my picture.

"AAAUUUUGGGGHHH!!" she screamed. "I look like a *dandelion!*"

That's how good of an artist I am: everybody always knows what it is.

"Dandelions are beautiful." I pulled her into the elevator, which has mirrors on all sides, so she could see.

Margaret shook her head. "For flowers, maybe. Not for people's heads. Besides, dandelions are

yellow, not brown. I look like a *dead* dandelion."
Then she brightened up a little. "Maybe *that* would
help. If my hair were yellow." Then she took a
long I-wish look at my hair in the mirror. "Or
red."

And for the first time that day, I saw Margaret
smile!

"I could do that for you, Margaret!" I told her.
"Oh, sure! I could make your hair red, just like
mine."

"How?" Margaret asked.

I'd been so happy to see Margaret smile that I'd
forgotten to figure out that part. But then a great
idea popped into my head. I am lucky that way:
great ideas are always popping into my head without me having to think them up. "My mother has
some special markers for her work. They color
over anything, and they stay there. Spinach got
hold of one and drew all over the walls and my

parents couldn't get it off. They had to paint the room over. That's how permanent those markers are."

Okay, fine, my brother's name is not really Spinach. But I got stuck with a name that is also a fruit, and it's not fair that he didn't. The only thing worse than a fruit name is a vegetable name, so that's what I think he should have. I have collected a lot of names for him.

"*Spinach* did that?" Margaret said. "The *easy* one?"

I squint-eyed her. "The *easy* one?"

"That's what my mother calls him. She says it's a good thing your parents got an easy one after you. Same thing in my family, but I'm the easy one. She says when there are two kids in a family, there's always an easy one and a hard one. I guess it's a rule."

"Oh, yeah," I said. "I knew that."

But I didn't.

"So how about those markers?" Margaret reminded me.

"Okay," I said. If the easy one could use them, I guessed the hard one could, too. "Let's go." And then we pressed *B* for basement and we rode down to my apartment.

I ran into the kitchen and climbed up onto the counter and grabbed the box of markers from where my mom had hidden them and jumped down. Before I left, I yelled to my mother in the living room, "Hi, Mom, everything went great at school, I was really paying attention, and now I'm going to play with Margaret because everything's fine with Margaret, no problems, 'bye." Just so she wouldn't worry.

And then I ran back out to Margaret in the elevator. She looked through the box and pulled out a marker named Flaming Sunset. Then she took off the cap and held the marker up against my hair. "Perfect," she said. "Let's go up to my apartment."

I'd forgotten about that part, too. "Is your mother still mad?" I asked.

"Yep. But she took three aspirin and went back to work. Only my brother is home."

So I said okay and we rode the elevator up to Margaret's apartment, even though I don't like Margaret's room.

One reason I don't like to go there is Mascara. Mascara always hides under Margaret's bed and hisses because he hates everyone except Margaret, but sometimes I can see his tail or one paw, and then I feel too sad because it reminds me of my old cat Polka Dottie who died.

Last year Polka had three kittens in my bureau drawer, which luckily I always leave open. My parents let me name them. Since I have discovered that the most exquisite words in the world are on labels you will find in a bathroom, I carried the kittens into the bathroom and looked around until I found them beautiful names. Fluoride and Laxative went to live with people who answered the *Free Kittens, Hurry!* ad my dad put in the paper, which was unfair to Polka because they were strangers. Then Margaret's mother said, "All right, Margaret, you can have a kitten as long as you take care of it yourself." And that was good, because at least Mascara would be living with someone Polka knew.

Except then Polka Dottie died. So now Margaret has a cat that's just fine and I don't.

But the main reason I don't like to go to Margaret's room is that it makes me feel itchy.

I feel itchy in Margaret's room because it looks like a magazine picture. Everything matches and everything is always exactly where it's supposed to be, in straight lines. Plus, nothing in her room is broken. And it's all clean—not a speck of dirt is allowed into her room. Actually, Margaret looks like a magazine picture, too. Her hair is always combed—well, it *used* to be—and her clothes always match and I think she probably sleeps in her bathtub, because I have never seen a single smudge of dirt on her.

I like her anyway, but it's not always easy.

"Remember the rules," Margaret said at her bedroom door.

While Margaret was looking under the bed for Mascara, I accidentally touched her lamp, which is a china poodle with an umbrella that Margaret calls a parasol because she is a show-off. Margaret turned around fast, but my hands jumped into my pockets even faster.

"All right," I said, "let's get going with the coloring." This is called Changing the Subject.

It is very hard to color hair with a marker, let me tell you. But I did it. I colored all of Margaret's hair chunks Flaming Sunset, and then another really great idea popped into my head and I drew Flaming Sunset curls all over her forehead and the back of her neck so her hair would look more like mine. It looked beautiful, like a giant tattoo of

tangled-up worms. When I am a grown-up, I will
have hundreds of tattoos.

Margaret looked in the mirror, then she looked
at my hair, then she looked in the mirror again and
she said, "Okay, good."

And then she told me she was getting bracelets
put on her teeth.

"You mean braces," I told her.

"No," she said. "Bracelets. They're a *special* kind of braces. They're *jewelry*."

"Oh," I said. "I knew that."

But I didn't. Okay, fine.

Later that night, when I was just at the hard part of falling asleep, which is lying in the dark trying not to think about pointy things, I heard the phone ring.

My dad said, "Hi, Susan," which is Margaret's mother's name, and then he didn't say anything for a long time. Then he said, "Now, Susan, let's just look at this calmly," and then he didn't say anything for another long time. And then he said "I'm sorry" seven times, which is two more times than he said it after he told my mother he thought her overalls were getting a little snug.

Next I heard him go into my brother's room, where my mom was putting Broccoli to bed, to say good night to him. Then I heard my parents whispering together as they walked down the hall to my room.

And I thought this would be an ideal time to practice pretending to be asleep.

I could feel them standing in my doorway, probably thinking, This hard one is a lot more trouble than the easy one. Then my dad said, "I really think Clementine was just trying to help her.

Margaret wanted hair like Clementine's. You know she's always been a little jealous."

That was the craziest thing I'd ever heard, because Margaret is perfect. But I couldn't tell them this, because an important part of pretending to be asleep is not talking.

I don't even want to think about the school part of Tuesday because it makes me too mad. "Margaret's mother sent a note to her teacher today that said 'watch out my daughter isn't left alone with Clementine'!" I told my mom as soon as I got home.

"Margaret's mother is upset right now," my mom said. "I guess I would be, too." Then she let me stir grape jelly into my milk to make me feel better.

I must have still been wearing a mad face when my dad walked in, because he just took one look at me and then handed me the key to the service elevator. My dad is the manager of our whole apartment building. He says that means all the people who live in the building, and even the pigeons, are the boss of him. But he has the keys to everything so I think that makes *him* the boss. And he understands that riding the service elevator calms me down when I'm mad.

Dad said, "Four times, Sport, that's all. And they're painting up on seven. If the painters need the elevator, you have to get right off."

So I rode up to seven to see if the painters needed any help. You never know.

And guess what I saw: three men painting the ceiling . . . *on stilts*! I am not even making this up!

"Need any help?" I asked. "Want me to put on some stilts?"

I guess they were being polite because they said,

"No, thanks, kiddo, we're all set," even though I could see they had a lot more to do.

So I rode the elevator exactly three more times and then I went back home. When I opened the door, I could hear my mom still talking to my dad about the note.

"How do you think that made her feel?" she said. "Imagine! As if our daughter is a common criminal!"

My dad snorted and said, "Well, that *is* insulting. There is absolutely nothing *common* about Clementine!"

And then my mom said, "That's not funny," and my dad

said, "Yes, it is. A little," and my mom said, "Okay, I guess it is. A little. But what are we going to do?"

And then I quickly closed the door and went back out before I could hear the answer in case it was "Let's trade her in for an easier kid."

I sat out in the lobby, waiting to get enough bravery to go up to the fifth floor and say *Sorry* to Margaret's mother, and ask her for a note that said "I do not think your daughter is a common criminal." Finally it came.

I didn't take the elevator to Margaret's apartment because I couldn't risk running into old Mrs. Jacobi. Every time I see her she hands me a five-dollar bill and says, "Run to the store and get me a box of Cheerios, dearie." I don't like to do it because then I have to bring it to her apartment on the top floor and talk to her while she counts the change and then hands me fifty cents. But if she asks me, I have to say yes because A) she is four hundred years old and I am polite, and B) I need the money because I am saving up to buy a gorilla and I bet they cost L-O-T-S, *lots*.

Anyway, I didn't have enough extra bravery to say *No, thanks,* to her too. So I walked up the back stairway—five times twelve stairs, which equals sixty—and I went to 5A and knocked.

Margaret's mother opened it and she just stood there looking like a magazine picture of a mother in a magazine picture of a living room.

I said, "Hi," and a bad surprise happened. Although I had never practiced it before, my voice sounded exactly like a common criminal's.

"You can't play with Margaret today, Clementine. She's spending the afternoon in her room, Thinking About the Consequences of Her Actions. Which is what you should be doing, too."

Okay, fine, she didn't actually say the last thing. But I could tell she was thinking it hard.

Behind her, Margaret's brother, Mitchell, leaned out from the kitchen doorway so I could see only his head and shoulders. Then, even though he is in Junior High and Should Know Better, he grabbed his hair and pretended to yank himself back into the kitchen. And I laughed even though I knew it was his own hand.

I do not think someone should be called "the hard one" if they make other people laugh.

"Clementine, there's nothing funny about this," said Margaret's mother.

I didn't tell her what was so funny and I didn't say any *Sorry*s and I didn't ask for a new note, in case I still had a common criminal's voice. I just ran down the hall.

This time I *did* take the elevator, because I was *hoping* I'd run into Mrs. Jacobi so I wouldn't have

to go right home. But I didn't, so I did. And when I opened the door to the apartment, I saw that our living room looked all wrong.

My mother was working at her drawing table. Suddenly I realized I had never seen a drawing table in a magazine picture of a living room.

I banged the door shut hard. "Margaret's mother always wears a dress." I didn't know I was going to say this.

"Margaret's mother works in a bank," my mother answered, still working on her drawing. "It might be a rule."

"Still," I said.

"I'm an artist, Clementine. I want to be comfortable. I get paint all over my clothes. I have to wear overalls or jeans. You know that, right?"

"Yes," I said. *Still.*

My mother put down her pencil and looked up then. "Clementine, do you sometimes wish you

had the kind of mother who worked in a bank and wore dresses?"

I nailed my mouth down so it couldn't say *Yes, maybe, sometimes,* and quick looked out the window, so my mother couldn't see my eyes thinking it.

Then my mother got up and looked out the window, too. Our apartment is at the basement level, which is halfway underground. This means the windows are right at the sidewalk height. So we both just stood there pretending to be extremely interested in all the feet passing by. What I was really doing was trying to imagine my mother in a dress. I guess that's what she was doing, too, because suddenly we both made corner-eyes at each other and then we burst out laughing and couldn't stop.

Finally my mother wiped her eyes and said, "Oh, come on. It wouldn't be *that* funny, would it?"

And I said, "Yep, it would."

And then I knew it was exactly the right time to tell her my secret. "When I grow up, I might be an artist."

And do you know what she said?

"Oh, Clementine, you already are! You may end up being something else, too—whatever you want to be—but you'll always be an artist. You just are."

And suddenly our living room looked exquisite with a drawing table in it! But now my fingers itched to be drawing, so I put on my jacket and went to the park to find something interesting to draw.

My dad says I am excellent at noticing interesting things. In fact, he says if noticing interesting

things were a sport, I would have a neckful of gold medals. He says that's a Very Good Sign for My Future. He says I could be a good detective, of course, but that noticing things is good for any career.

My mom says that means I could be a good artist, too.

Or a writer. Last year a writer came to my school and said, *Pay Attention!* But she didn't mean to the teacher, she meant pay attention to what's going on around you, so you can write about it. Then she looked exactly at me and said to notice the good stuff and write it down so you don't forget it.

So, even though I'm not going to be a writer— too much sitting still—I notice interesting things and write them down. I draw them, too.

In the park, I saw something great right away: a

woman eating lentils from a thermos . . . with a toothbrush! Even though she had a fork right there, which she was using to eat her salad!

So I asked the lady if I could draw a picture of the lentils on her toothbrush and she said, "Sure," so I did and here it is:

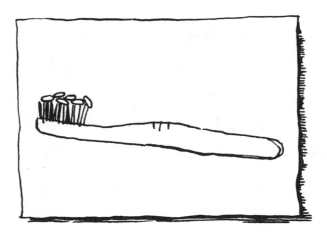

As soon as I got home I wrote it all down and asked my mom if we could have lentils for dinner.

"You hate lentils, Clementine," my mother reminded me.

"Well, I think I've been eating them wrong," I said.

So we had lentils and I ate them the new way and guess what? It worked. The lentils stuck on the bristles and didn't slide off like with a fork. So I got lots and lots of lentils in my mouth.

Which was a bad thing because I hate lentils.

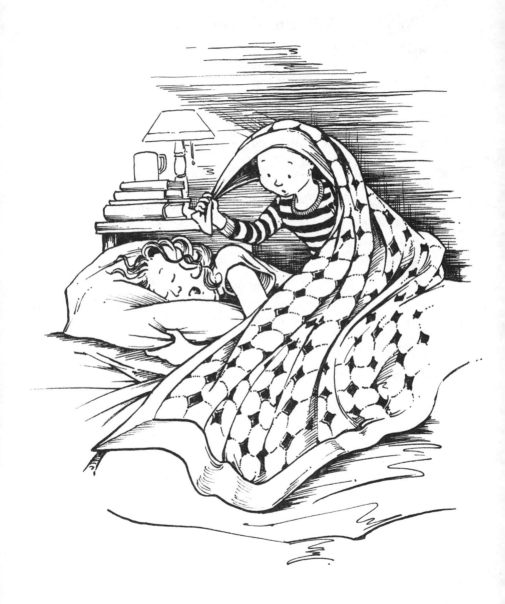

CHAPTER

4

"I'd better not go to school today," I told my mom on Wednesday as soon as I woke her up. "I have cracked toes." I put my foot right up on the pillow next to her face so she could see without getting up. This is called Being Thoughtful.

"Nope," she said, without even opening her eyes to see if it was true.

"Well, that's not all," I said. "I also have the heartbreak of sore irises."

"Nope," she said again, and she still didn't open her eyes.

"Actually, I think I have arthritis," I said. "Mrs.

Jacobi was breathing on me in the elevator the other day, and I must have caught it."

"Oh, please," she said, but this time she opened one eye. And then she made exactly the sound Polka Dottie used to make when she had a hairball.

I grabbed the corner of the quilt and covered my head, but my mom pulled it off again. She took my head in her hands and twisted it around to see all the sides. Too hard, like I wasn't inside it.

"You've cut off all your hair!" she said. "You've

cut off all your beautiful hair! What on earth were you *thinking*, Clementine?"

"I wanted to make Margaret feel better," I explained. "I didn't want her to be the only one! But I forgot: Margaret's not going to school today. She has an appointment at the orthodentist's to have bracelets put on her teeth."

Mom groaned and closed her eyes again. But she slid over and made room for me on the warm part of her sheets.

I climbed in and took a big sniff. My mom's part of the bed smells like cinnamon rolls. My dad's part smells like pinecones. Right in the middle it's all mixed up perfectly—that's my favorite place to be. But this morning, Dad was already off to fight in The Great Pigeon War and it was fine just being on the cinnamon-roll part.

My mom put her arm around me. "Oh. So now *you'll* be the only one," she said. "I'm sorry, honey, but you can't stay home. You have to go and face the music."

So I had to go to school, which almost turned out to be a very bad mistake, because I almost had to go to the hospital with the ambulance and the sirens and everything!

It happened in the principal's office, when my teacher sent me there to have a little chat about sitting still.

When I walked in, Principal Rice made the hair-ball sound, too. "Clementine!" she gulped. "What have you *done?* You've chopped off your hair!"

I was glad she'd answered her question so I didn't have to. "Wow," I said instead. "*Clementine* and *Rice*! We both have food names!"

Mrs. Rice sealed her lips tight like she was afraid her teeth were going to run away. Then she opened up the note from my teacher.

"I can't help it," I said, before she could start the little chat. "I'm allergic to sitting still."

"Nobody is allergic to sitting still, Clementine," she said.

"I am," I said. "My brother is allergic to peanuts. If he eats one he gets all itchy and swelled up and he can't breathe right. If I try to sit still I get all itchy and swelled up and I can't breathe right. So that means I'm allergic to sitting still."

Mrs. Rice squeezed her eyes shut and rubbed her forehead. I happen to know this means *This idea is so bad it's giving me a headache*, because it's the face I make when my mother tells me to visit Mrs. Jacobi. The face never works for me.

"Plus," I explained, "if my brother eats even one tiny peanut he might have to go to the hospital with the ambulance and sirens and everything!

So if I sit still for even one minute . . . Uh-oh!" I gave my body an extra little jiggle just to stay safe. "Phew!" I said. "That was close!"

Principal Rice sighed like a leaky balloon. "Clementine, do you think when you're in class you could just try to wiggle a little more quietly from now on?"

I asked my body about this and it said, "Sure," so I told it to Mrs. Rice. "Sure," I said.

"Good," she said. "Now, as long as you're here, how about we discuss your hair?"

Thinking about my hair made me think about Margaret. Thinking about Margaret made me remember about her getting bracelets on her teeth.

I want bracelets on my teeth more than anything. But then I had a bad thought: what if they had pointy edges?

I didn't want to have any pointy things stuck in my mind to worry me all day, so I looked out the window, because the only way to erase pointy things is with round things, and clouds are good for that. Right away I saw a cloud that would make a wonderful tattoo: it looked exactly like a dog, if dogs had only two legs—on the top, not the bottom. I am not allowed to have tattoos yet— which is unfair—so for now, I just draw things on my arms so I don't forget them. But I didn't have a pen. I looked around the desk to see if Mrs. Rice had a tattoo-drawing pen, and suddenly I realized something very suspicious: *I had never seen Mrs. Rice's arms!* They were always in principal sleeves!

"Do you have a tattoo?" I asked. "Can I see it?"

"What?" Mrs. Rice asked. "Clementine, we were talking about your hair!"

"That was a long time ago," I reminded her. I added a kind smile, because it's not her fault she has trouble paying attention.

CHAPTER

5

As soon as I got home, I started watching for Margaret's feet. From my kitchen window I can see the sidewalk in front of the lobby doors. Since I have memorized all the shoes of everybody who lives in our building, I always know who's coming in or going out. I might be a detective when I grow up.

I waited and I waited and I waited, which is the hardest thing in the world. Especially when you have a hot head, which I did, because my mother made me wear my winter hat so she didn't have to look at my chopped-off hair. Finally I saw Margaret's purple sneakers, and I ran up to meet her in the lobby.

"Let me see."

Margaret pulled her lips out of the way so I could see all of her teeth.

Margaret's mouth was the most beautiful place I have ever seen. It was even more beautiful than Disneyland, Sleeping Beauty's Castle, which I am going to visit when I am ten. Every tooth had its own sparkly silver bracelet and there were little blue bits sprinkled around like tiny presents.

"They're rubber bands," Margaret said. "Every month I'll go in and get them changed and they'll give me different colors. Whatever I want."

That gave me such a good idea.

I pulled off my hat to show Margaret that she wasn't the only one, and that made her happy. Then I told her my good idea. "You can pick the color of my new hair. Whatever color you want. You can draw it on my head." That made her even happier.

"Those markers are still in my room. Let's go," she said.

"Is your mother still mad?" I asked.

"Yep. But she's going to a movie with Alan this afternoon."

Alan is Margaret's mother's "special friend," which is the grown-ups' word for boyfriend.

So we went up to her apartment. Mitchell was there, watching TV. When he saw my hair, he grabbed his chest and fell off the couch, pretending to have a heart attack. Then he smacked his forehead and said, "You guys are unbelievable. Absolutely unbelievable," even though he is older

and doesn't have to be so nice to us. I think he likes me.

Margaret glared at him. Then she jabbed her elbow into my side and so I glared at him, too, even though I didn't know why we were doing that. I'm not so sure Margaret is the easy one in that family.

She dragged me into her room. "I can't wait for summer," she growled. "My mother's finally going to get rid of him."

"You mean baseball camp? He wants to go, Margaret. That's not getting rid of someone."

Margaret gave me her I'm-in-fourth-grade-and-you're-not look. "Good-bye and good riddance," she muttered.

Then she got out my mother's markers. They were all still there and they looked exactly the same, with none of the caps chewed up. I don't know how Margaret does that. She picked a bright green one and colored my hair and then drew some curls on my forehead and neck.

"No pointy lines," I reminded her. "Just round ones."

Thinking about pointy lines made me wonder about Margaret's bracelets again. "How do they feel? I bet they're full of pointy parts."

"Nope, they feel like *heaven*," Margaret said. "No pointy parts at all. They're as soft as rabbit ears. *Baby* rabbit ears. Too bad you can't have them." She kept her lips stretched out of the way to show me her teeth the whole time she talked, so it was kind of hard to understand her.

But I did.

"I'm getting them, too," I said. "Next week."

Then I pulled my hat back on and ran down to my apartment quick to make this be a non-lie.

"I need bracelets on my teeth," I told my mom. "They're beautiful and they feel wonderful."

"First of all," my mother said, "they don't feel wonderful. Not in the beginning, anyway. Margaret's mother stopped in earlier, asking if we had any medicine left over from when your brother was teething. She told me Margaret cried all the way home."

That Margaret.

"Well, I still want them. Next week."

"And second of all, you don't need them. Your teeth are straight enough."

Which is the most unfair thing I have ever heard.

"I can feel them bending," I said. And suddenly I could. "So we'd better make that appointment."

Then, before my mom could get to third of all, which is usually the worst one, we heard my brother waking up from his nap.

"I'm coming, Radish," I called to him.

"Go for a wok?" he asked, when I came into his room.

"You're lucky to have me for a big sister," I told him. I have to remind him of this every day, because he forgets. We went into the kitchen and I got out the wok. "Nobody invented this trick for me when I was little."

Then he climbed into the wok and grabbed the handles and I gave him a really good spin. He went whirling around, bumping into the cabinets, and then he got out and walked wobbly until he fell

over, which he thinks is the funniest thing in the world.

"Again!" he yelled.

But I didn't spin him again, because he throws up on the second ride and somebody has to clean it up which is N-O-T, *not* me. This is called Being Responsible.

He came over to me and pulled off my hat and pointed to my head. "Green?"

And I thought about something.

First Margaret had straight brown hair, and we didn't look alike. Then we cut it off and colored it red, so we sort of did. Then she got bracelets on her teeth, which meant we didn't look alike. But soon her teeth would be straight, and we would. Except now I had a green head.

What if we never looked alike?

What if we did?

CHAPTER
6

Thursday morning I woke up with a spectacularful idea. I am lucky that way—spectacularful ideas are always sproinging up in my brain. The secret thing I know about ideas is that once they sproing into your head you have to grab them fast, or else they get bored and bounce away. So I called Margaret and told her I had a good surprise for her and we needed to sit in the backseat of the bus.

It is unfair that sometimes even spectacularful ideas don't work out. It is also unfair that bus drivers are allowed to send you to the principal's office.

"It's not my fault," I explained to Principal Rice before she could say any of those Clementine-why-did-you's. "Margaret has very slippery head skin."

Mrs. Rice fell into her chair, hard. She clapped her hands over her ears and squeezed like her brains were trying to jump out. Part of me wanted to see something like that, but most of me said, Not today, thanks!

"Margaret's slippery head skin is *not* the problem," she said. "The problem is that you tried to glue your own hair onto Margaret's head. You've been having *lots* of problems this week. First you cut off Margaret's hair. Then you colored her head. Yesterday you cut off your own hair and colored your own head. And today this. Clementine, what's going on between you and Margaret?"

"How do you spell nitrogen?" I asked Mrs. Rice. Sometimes grown-ups get distracted if you ask them school things.

But Mrs. Rice just spelled nitrogen for me and went right back to the Margaret thing. "Are you angry with her?"

"*NO!*" I said. Okay, fine, I yelled it. But I didn't know I was going to yell it. And I couldn't stop my yelling voice. "HERE IS HOW GOOD OF A FRIEND I AM TO MARGARET: I'M NOT EVEN MAD AT HER FOR LAST WEEK AT MY PARTY, EVEN THOUGH SHE BREATHED ON THE M&M ROCKS IN THE BACK OF THE DUMP TRUCK, WHICH WAS THE BEST PART OF MY CAKE, AND THEN SHE SAT ON MY SPARKLE-GLITTER PAINT SET, WHICH WAS MY BEST PRESENT, AND SAID IT WAS AN ACCIDENT BUT I DON'T THINK SO, AND NOW SHE'S TRYING TO LOOK LIKE ME EXCEPT SHE GETS TO HAVE BRACELETS AND I DON'T."

"Oh," said Principal Rice. And then she didn't say anything at all, just looked at me, which is the worst thing of all that can happen to you in the principal's office. I sat there swinging my legs back and forth like crazy for three hundred hours and then I said, "Can I be done here now?"

And she said, "Okay, fine."

Margaret's mother let her come over to play after school.

"Does this mean she's all done being mad at me?" I asked.

"No. She just doesn't think there's anything left for you to do to my head. Besides, she says I'm nine years old and I should be able to protect my own head."

Then I told her some good news I had just thought up.

"I am nine years old now, too."

"No, you're not. You're eight," she said. "I came to your birthday last week."

Which I remembered.

"No," I explained. "I was eight at my party. Nine comes *after* eight, and it is *after* my party, so now I am nine. And that means we're the same age!"

"That's ridiculous!" yelled Margaret. "I'm almost *ten* and you're *eight*! You are not nine!" She tried to flip her hair, which didn't work so well without actual hair, and her head got even redder under the scrubbed-off marker.

"Yes, I am," I told her. "I'm in the gifted class for math, so I understand about numbers."

Then Margaret left and slammed my door. That Margaret—after all I've done for her, helping her fix her stupid hair!

I followed her into the lobby and yelled, "You shouldn't have breathed on my cake and sat on my present and I don't want you to look like me!"

But she didn't even turn around, so now I had nobody to play with for the rest of my life. But I didn't care because I was nine.

Or maybe I was just after-eight, okay, fine.

Being after-eight reminded me that I hadn't checked yet that day to see if I'd started growing a beard, so I ran to the bathroom. While I was there I accidentally climbed onto the toilet seat to look out the window into the side alley to see if Margaret went out there. I didn't see her, but I didn't care. Especially when I looked in the mirror and saw that I had started growing a nice brown beard on one cheek!

"Hey, Bill!" I yelled. Bill is my dad's for-other-people name. "Where's your razor?"

Dad came skidding into the bathroom so fast I thought his feet might be on fire, but they weren't. I showed him my beard.

Dad squinted and sniffed my cheek. "That's not a beard, Clementine," he sighed. "That's chocolate frosting. As a matter of fact, that smells exactly like the kind of chocolate frosting that your mother put on the cake she made for her book club, which nobody was supposed to touch. Now isn't that a coincidence?"

Okay, fine.

I wiped off the frosting and underneath was a very mad face.

"Clementine," my dad said, "you know girls don't grow beards."

"What about The Amazing Bearded Lady at the circus? What about that, huh?"

"Clementine, I've told you a hundred times: you can't grow a beard."

"So Rutabaga gets to have one like yours some day? Down to his knees if he wants? And I don't? That's not fair." Which I have told *him* a hundred times.

"First of all, your brother's name isn't Rutabaga," Dad said. "Second of all . . . well, never mind. Maybe today isn't the time to talk about what's fair."

My dad and I looked at my mad mirror face with the green-markered top for a long time.

"I sure am having a lot of trouble with hair these days," I whispered.

"I know, Sport," Dad said. Then he hugged me. Usually this squeezes the mad right out of me. But that time it just mixed it all up with feeling sad and lucky, which was extremely confusing.

"Hey," my dad said. "Have you got a little time to spare?"

I squint-eyed him: it depended.

"The Great Pigeon War," he said. "It's time for evening maneuvers. I could use someone like you on the front lines tonight. Someone with fresh ideas. I'm running a little low on them myself."

I said okay, and my dad and I put on our raincoats and went outside.

First he got out the hose, which he calls the heavy artillery. Then he sprayed off the front steps and the sidewalk in front of the lobby doors. Last, he pointed the hose at the pigeons covering the ledges and windowsills and balconies and roofs of the front of our building. He sprayed them until they all flew away. That's the best part, because when a million pigeons take off at the same time right above you, you can feel their wing beats exploding inside you, like fireworks.

My dad handed me the hose. "Want to clean the lion?"

Which, of course, I did. The carved lion above the front door has really pointy teeth, but I'm not afraid of him because he's using those teeth to

protect us. Plus, he's just stone. I sprayed him with
the hose until he was all shiny in the streetlights.

"You know, Dad," I pointed out, "it's not really
the pigeons you're at war with. The pigeons aren't
the enemy."

"What are you talking about?" he asked. "It's my job to keep the building looking nice, especially the entrance. You've seen what those pigeons do."

"Exactly," I said. "The pigeons are fine. It's their mess you hate."

"Well, okay, that's true," my dad said. "I'm actually at war with pigeon splat. You got any ideas how to get rid of the pigeon splat without getting rid of the pigeons?"

"How about diapers?" I suggested. "We could wait until all the pigeons are asleep, then sneak up and put little diapers on them!"

"Brilliant!" my dad cried. "See? That's what I'm talking about. I can always count on you to see things from a new angle. I'm going to make you a captain!"

"You made me a captain last week. For the idea about charging them rent," I reminded him.

"You can be a sergeant then," he promised.

"Never mind," I said. "Who would change all those diapers every day? Not me."

"Hmmmm," Dad said, "excellent point. Back to the drawing board, Sport."

Then we just sat there together watching the pigeons flock back to our building for the night. We listened to them cooing above us, sounding like a million old ladies with secrets.

"What are we going to do?" I asked. "I mean for real?"

CHAPTER

7

I knew Friday was going to be a bad day right from the beginning, because there were clear parts in my eggs.

"I can't eat eggs if they have clear parts," I reminded my mother.

"Eat around them," she said. "Just eat the yellow parts and the white parts."

But I couldn't because the clear parts had touched the yellow parts and the white parts. So all I had was toast.

"Have you got all your stuff?" my dad asked as I was leaving.

"Of course," I said. "Right in my backpack." But when I went to show him my homework— three sentences about the planet Saturn, which I had decorated with a picture of some squirrels I'd seen in the park—it wasn't there!

"Better go check The Black Hole," he said.

I gave my dad a "that's-not-funny" look, but I went back into my room to check. The Black Hole is what my dad calls the place under my bed. He says things mysteriously disappear there. I do not think fathers should be comedians.

My homework paper was not under my bed.

And the rest of the day got worse.

On the bus, Margaret walked right past our usual seat and sat down next to Amanda-Lee, even though all Amanda-Lee can talk about is going to the mall, which is boring. Plus, anyone with a name as beautiful as Amanda-Lee probably made it up.

Then, as soon as I got to school, the teacher said, "The following students are excused from recess so they can catch up on their journal writing," and I was one of the following students.

Three times during journal writing the teacher said, "Clementine, you need to pay attention." And every time he said it, I *was* paying attention. I was paying attention out the window where the fourth-graders were playing Pickle in the Middle. Whenever the ball came anywhere near Margaret and Amanda-Lee, they grabbed each other and shrieked like they were being murdered, which everyone knows means "We are best friends!"

When my teacher moved my seat away from the window I was G-L-A-D, *glad*. And I wrote all over my journal page, I DON'T CARE! so hard my pencil broke.

When I got home from school, I was planning on going straight to my room to draw a picture of me with a new best friend. But my dad was putting on his raincoat and it was not raining out.

"Fighting pigeons is not for the weak-hearted," he said. "It takes superhuman courage. And resourcefulness and cleverness."

When my dad talks like this it means he has a new idea. "You have another battle plan?" I asked.

"Yup," he answered. "And it's a doozy. I'll probably be promoted to general for this one."

"You already are the general, remember?"

"Oh, right. I'm so modest I sometimes forget. Well, I bet I get the Medal of Honor."

"Dad."

"I might even be knighted for this one."

"*Dad!*" I said. Sometimes my dad needs help staying serious. "So what *is* the new battle plan?"

My dad looked around, like he thought there might be spies sneaking up on us. Then he bent over and whispered in my ear. "Psychological warfare!"

This sounded like a good one, so I followed him out and sat on the steps to watch. I could do that drawing later.

First my dad hosed off the sidewalk, then sprayed the pigeons until they flew away. All the time he was muttering things like "Oh, they're crafty all right. But I'm craftier!" and "It's a little-known fact that pigeons were the eighth deadly plague to visit Egypt."

Then he pulled a brown plastic owl from a bag. He got a ladder and climbed up and put the owl right on top of the lion's head over the lobby door.

I asked him what that was for.

"The pigeons will take one look at that owl, and then they'll head for the hills. Well, for another building. Pigeons are deathly afraid of owls. Yep, I'll probably be knighted."

"It's plastic," I reminded him.

"But the pigeons don't know that. That's the brilliance of my plan."

I didn't see what was so brilliant. I didn't see how a little plastic owl was going to frighten off a flock of pigeons who fought over who would get to sit on the head of a roaring lion.

And while we stood there, Dad admiring his brilliant battle plan and me worrying about it, the pigeons came back. They settled on their regular perches all over the front of our building, except for a few who decided to sit on the owl's head.

What my dad needed was something real.

"Polka Dottie would have scared them off."

Dad put the ladder and his raincoat away and came over and sat beside me. "You still miss her, don't you, Sport."

I nodded. "I miss seeing her when I get home from school. I miss patting her where her fur was

so soft under her neck. I miss hearing her purr when I fall asleep. I even miss the smell of her cat food."

"That's a lot of missing," my dad said.

"And she would have scared off those pigeons, wouldn't she?"

"Absolutely. That was one terrifying cat."

"Dad. She would have been terrifying *to pigeons*," I said. And then I had one of the most astoundishing ideas of my whole career.

I jumped up and gave my dad a kiss right where his beard stops being crunchy. Then I ran back into the apartment, went to my bedroom, and reached under the mattress where I keep my favorite picture of Polka.

Then I ran to the copy shop at the corner.

"Can you make this bigger?" I asked.

"How big do you want it?" the clerk asked back.

I took out my wallet and laid all my birthday

money on the counter. "How big can you make it for this much?"

The clerk counted my money and thought for a minute. "I can make that cat the size of a German shepherd for that much money."

"Perfect," I said.

Then he took the money and the picture of Polka and told me to come back the next day at four.

I ran home and let myself into the apartment. My dad and mom were in the kitchen.

"... *one* left," my dad said.

"One's all we need," said my mom. "Do you think we should do it?"

"I think so," my dad answered. "I think it's time."

"Okay," my mom said. "I'll call tomorrow."

One's all we need?! I slammed the door behind me so they would know I was there. If they were talking about getting rid of me so they'd only have one kid—the easy one—I wanted them to s-t-o-p, *stop*. Not that I was worried. They probably weren't even talking about me anyway.

"Shhhh!" my dad said. "She's home."

Okay, fine, I was worried.

CHAPTER
8

Here is a secret good thing: Sometimes I like journal writing at school because I can remind myself of things I might forget when I'm a grown-up. Like that I plan to smoke cigars. And I do *not* plan to get married. Cigars, yes; husband, no. What if I forget these things?

One more thing to remember when I am old: if I ever do get married, which I will *not*, I will only have one kid. The first one. She is plenty good enough. Even if she's the hard one.

Nope, no need for another kid, even if he's the easy one. Although thinking about my brother and thinking about my journal gave me an astound-ishing idea on Saturday.

Last week Turnip had to get a shot at the doctor's and he was so mad about it my parents let him rent a video and eat Gummi Worms even though they are usually the *Sesame Street*–and-carrot-sticks kind of parents. So I pretended I had to write in my journal even though I didn't because it was the weekend, and I pretended I was mad about it so my parents would feel sorry for me, too.

As soon as they came into the room I scringed my eyebrows down like arrows and stuck my bottom teeth out as far as they could go. Here is a picture of that:

If my teeth were pointier I would have looked *fierce*, like our stone lion. Still, see how mad I looked?

But guess what my parents did? Nothing. Because they are not so good at paying attention.

"Excuse me," I said. "I am very mad about this journal. May I please have some Gummi Worms and a video?"

They stared at me like I had spoken in the secret language Margaret and I use, which I was almost sure I had not.

"You let Zucchini have Gummi Worms and a video when he was mad about his shot," I reminded them.

"First of all," my mother said, "your brother's name isn't Zucchini. Second of all, he's three years old."

"And third of all," my father said, "considering

all the trouble you got into this week, I don't think it's quite the time for special treats, do you?"

"Okay, fine," I said.

But it wasn't.

In the afternoon, my mom had to go to her yoga class and my brother had to go to his Saturday play group. My dad was around, but he was up on the second floor taking care of a "plumbing issue." Usually on Saturday afternoons Margaret and I play together, but now Margaret was not my friend anymore. So I had nothing to do, not even eat Gummi Worms and watch a video, for three whole hours until I could go back to get the big Polka picture.

Then I realized I didn't exactly know where I should put the picture once I got it.

What I needed was one of the top windows, right in the middle of the building, where it would scare off the pigeons. Margaret's apartment was on the fifth floor, but I didn't think Margaret's mother was about to let a common criminal use her window. The man who lives on the sixth floor smells like mothballs, so I never visit him. The people who live on the seventh floor were away on vacation while their apartment got painted.

Which reminded me.

I flew up to the seventh floor to see if the painters wanted help yet. Nobody answered the apartment door when I knocked, but the painters' stilts and all their brushes and paint cans were out in the hall. The hall hadn't been painted yet, which gave me a great idea: I could do it for them! Then, when they got back on Monday, they'd smack their foreheads and make "Wow! I must be dreaming!" faces. They'd wonder who had done such a great thing until I went up and told them, "Oh, it was just me."

I was smiling about all this while I strapped the stilts onto my legs. But when I tried to stand up, I fell right over. I tried again, and I fell right over again.

Twenty-nine times. Which was plenty, believe me, so I was all done being there.

On the way down, the elevator stopped at the fifth floor. I got a little bit excited when Margaret got in and smiled at me, but then one second later that Amanda-Lee got in too.

"Hi, Clementine. We're going to the mall," Margaret said.

I turned around and pretended to be very busy pushing all the buttons until they got off. Then I went to my room and drew a picture of me at the mall with *a lot* of new best friends.

Finally it was time to go to the copy shop, and I ran all the way, even though I probably had two broken legs from all that falling.

When the clerk brought out the picture of Polka Dottie, my heart hurt so much I couldn't breathe for a minute. She looked so beautiful that big, and I missed her so much. I quick sucked in some air so I wouldn't faint and then I said, "Thank you," and took Polka home, being careful not to fold her, because she would have hated that.

When I got to my building, I looked up through all the pigeons. At the very top of the building was old Mrs. Jacobi's apartment. I tucked the big picture of Polka under my arm, took the elevator to the eighth floor, and knocked on Mrs. Jacobi's door.

"Can I put this in your window?" I asked. "The one in the middle of your living room?"

Mrs. Jacobi said, "Why, certainly, dearie!" without even asking why, and suddenly she didn't look so old or so boring.

I went to the window and opened it. When I looked down, I could see the backs of a million cooing pigeons. They covered every windowsill, every balcony, every ledge, every brick that stuck out even an inch. In between, I could see the sidewalk in front of the building, still wet from my dad's washing. I guessed this was what my dad meant about seeing things from a different angle, but I didn't understand how it could help.

Mrs. Jacobi came over beside me and shook half a box of Cheerios onto the windowsill. The pigeons flapped up in one huge gray cloud.

And my brain snapped, HEY!!
HEY!!

I ran out of Mrs. Jacobi's apartment and all the way down to my own—eight times twelve stairs, which equals ninety-six.

"Dad!" I yelled. "What if the pigeons lived on
the side of the building, instead of in the front?
Would that be okay?"

"That would be great," my dad said. "A miracle. Except, of course, first you'd have to convince a million pigeons to move."

"But if I could, would that solve the problem? You wouldn't care if they messed all over the sidewalk in the side alley?"

"Nope, not a bit. Nobody uses it. That alley could be knee-deep in pigeon splat, and nobody would even notice. Fire away, I'd say."

And then I ran all the way back up the stairs to Mrs. Jacobi's apartment and went right inside since the door was still open—because that's how fast I was!

"I'll run for your Cheerios every week," I told her. "You won't even have to ask me. Every day, if you want. But will you stop feeding the pigeons from here? Will you feed them from a side window instead?"

I took her into the dining room and showed her a perfect place. "Let's start today," I said, and I sprinkled out the rest of the box of Cheerios. And even though pigeons have teeny tiny bird brains, they got the message pretty quick because right away a big flock of them flapped over.

And it was even better for Mrs. Jacobi because this was her dining room, so now she could see those pigeons eating when she was eating!

And then I was all done being there, so I ran back home to tell my dad the good news.

He and my mom were in the kitchen starting dinner so I told them and I told them and I told them! And my dad kept saying "Way to *go*, Sport!" and my mom kept saying "Thank goodness! Now you don't have to spend your life cleaning up after those pigeons!"

They were *SO* happy! But my parents were

sneaky, too. Somehow, while I was telling them about Mrs. Jacobi, one of them slipped me a colander of green beans and brainwashed me into snapping them.

I didn't really care, though. Seeing the "Wow!

I must be dreaming!" faces on my parents was even better than it would have been seeing them on the painters.

Unfortunately, they didn't have those faces very long.

After dinner, my mother said she'd better get a little work done. Then she went to the cupboard to get her special markers. Which were still in Margaret's room.

"You used my . . . not the permanent . . . those are for . . . what were you . . . ?!"

It's a very bad sign when my mother can't finish her sentences.

"They're at Margaret's," I told her. "They're fine—not even chewed on. I'll go get them. . . ."

"Oh, no," said my father. "*We'll* go get them. I think it's time we had a talk with Margaret's mother anyway. You'll go sit in your room and think about things."

So I went to my room and thought about things. Like Margaret's mother explaining to my parents about the "easy one-hard one" rule.

CHAPTER

9

"I cannot look at your green head for one more day," my mom said as soon as I woke up Sunday morning.

So right after breakfast she took me into the kitchen and started scrubbing my head with scouring powder and saying things I have never heard a TV mother say. She scrubbed so hard she probably made a hole right through my head skin and my head bone, and now everybody can see right into my brains and I'd better not do any more cartwheels.

All the time, I watched out the kitchen window for Margaret's feet.

"Margaret's brother is not my special friend," I told my mother this in case she thought I was watching out for Mitchell's feet which I was not, because he's not my special friend.

My mother kept on scrubbing and all she said was "That's nice," which is what grown-ups say when they're not paying attention to you.

Suddenly, with my amazing corner-eyes I saw what my dad was reading to my brother in the living room.

"Stop!" I yelled. Then I flew over and jumped on his lap and slammed the book shut just in time.

"Lima Bean is *little*, Dad!" I reminded him. "He'd get scared of those shoes!"

"First of all, your brother's name isn't Lima Bean," said my dad. "And second of all, *what* shoes, Clementine?"

I told you he was not so good at paying attention—those shoes are pretty hard to miss.

"The pointy green ones on the bear," I whispered. "Page fourteen."

Which I know because, okay, fine, I look at that page a lot. Some days I like to scare myself. Today was not one of those days, though.

"It's just a picture, Sport," Dad said. "It's not real. Do you want to try looking at it with me right here?"

"NO!" I yelled. And then I was mad because now those pointy shoes were stuck in my head, going to worry me all day. I jumped off my dad's lap and ran back into the kitchen, because I have discovered that lots of foods are round. Cookies, hamburgers, pizzas, doughnuts, cupcakes, apples— you name it, all the good stuff is round.

I grabbed two slices of bologna and I bit them into a pair of glasses, which is a trick I invented and only I know and now you will, too. Fold a slice of bologna in half and then bite right in the middle of the flat side. Do it again. Then slap the circles over your eyes and you have bologna glasses! Here is a picture of that:

And then because I am so good of a sister and okay, fine, because I was still hungry, I made a pair for my brother, too.

"Here, Pea Pod," I said, climbing back onto my dad's lap and slapping my brother's pair onto his eyes. "Put on your glasses."

My brother started laughing so hard he spit up his breakfast waffles and my parents said, *"Clem-en-tine, please!"* at exactly the same time, which I think they practice at night when I am asleep, but they were laughing, too.

And suddenly it was a pretty good day in spite of the hole scrubbed into my head.

The good-day feeling made me think about all the bad-day feelings I'd been having this week, and that made me think about Margaret, and then the best idea of all sproinged right into my brain.

Because I am so good at paying attention, I know all the things that Margaret likes. So I ran around my apartment gathering them up:

Polka Dottie's flea collar, because Margaret loved my old cat.

Pepperoni, because that's the only kind of pizza I have ever seen her eat.

The red shoes Margaret makes me put on Barbie every time we play.

A blue jay feather from my collection, because her favorite color is blue.

Some M&M's, because she breathed on mine.

My charm bracelet, because she always makes I-wish eyes at it.

Lace ripped from my party socks, because I borrowed them from Margaret one time and I forgot to tell her.

Pink sparkle nail polish, because she tried to borrow it from me but I caught her.

A dead bumblebee—I don't know why.

The rest of the red curly hair I cut off, because that's how we got into all this trouble in the first place.

Then I got my mother's favorite hat, a big bottle of glue, and my dad's aftershave, which Margaret and I love to squirt all over us because it has such a heavenly aroma.

I glued and I glued and I glued, and I squirted and I squirted and I squirted. And I smiled. Then I ran out and guess who I met in the elevator?

Margaret! Without Amanda-Lee!

"I have something for you," we both said at exactly the same time, which we have never practiced before. Then I handed her the Margaret hat and she handed me a bag. Inside was a brand-new, not-sat-on, Sparkle-Glitter Paint Set.

"I got it at the mall," Margaret said. Then, without even a grown-up telling her to, she told me she was sorry she was mean to me at my birthday.

"I'm sorry about your hair," I said.

"Okay, fine," we both said.

And it was. For about one minute.

"I have to go," Margaret said. "I'll see you tonight."

"Yep. See you tonight," I said. Then I said, "Um . . . what's tonight?"

"The party. Your parents invited us."

"Oh, right," I said. "I knew that." But I didn't. Uh-oh.

If my parents were having a party and I didn't know about it, that meant it was a surprise party. Surprise parties are either for birthdays or going-aways.

It wasn't my birthday anymore.

I raced back to my apartment. My parents were in their bedroom.

"That's right, a chocolate cake with vanilla frosting," my mom was saying to someone on the phone. "'Good-bye and Good Riddance!' should be in red icing."

"Make sure they spell her name right," I heard my dad say.

Then my mom spelled C-L-E-M-E-N-T-I-N-E, and said she'd be over to pick it up soon.

There wasn't much time.

"Well, I guess I'll go clean my room," I said,

extra loud, as I walked through the living room. I tried to make it sound as if these words were used to coming out of my mouth. "Yep, I'll just be cleaning like crazy this afternoon."

My dad came out and squinted at me, and then sat down to read his *Boston Globe*. My mother just glanced at me as she passed by to help my brother with his puzzle.

"Maybe when I'm done, I'll clean Radish's room, too," I tried. "And then I'll do my homework. If you need me to help with anything, or solve any more problems like The Great Pigeon War, just come and get me."

"Okay, Clementine," my parents said. But they didn't even look up this time.

So it was probably too late. Just in case it wasn't, I got the spray bottle of cleaner and some paper towels, because even though I have never actually cleaned my room, I know that's the first step.

Except I didn't know what to do next. I wanted my room to look like Margaret's, like a magazine picture, but I didn't know how to do it.

The problem was, everything already looked great to me.

Luckily, I knew what my parents would like me to clean.

I dragged out everything from The Black Hole and piled it on top of my bed. And you would not believe how much stuff came out!

Four shoes, three brushes, and too many hair clips to count. Socks, a really crunchy Easter Peep, and the top hat that had been missing from the Monopoly game for two years. A Mr. Potato Head nose, three library books, my book report due last Monday, and Friday's Saturn sentences. Some more socks. A Halloween mask, the skirt I

pretended I lost, two flashlights, a mitten. A green plastic trapezoid, a "Taking it Easy in the Everglades" snow globe, half a button, Polka Dottie's favorite rubber mouse. Mom's yoga video and Dad's needle-nosed pliers. Forty-five cents. Even more socks.

I got the things all piled up on my bed, and even though they looked fine to me, I started to clean them. I squirted everything with lots of cleaner and rubbed hard with paper towels.

I squirted and I rubbed all afternoon. It started to get dark outside. But nothing got cleaner. Everything just got wetter. And covered with glumps of wet paper towel. Suddenly my eyes were crying and they wouldn't stop.

And that's when my parents came in.

"I just got some cleaner in my eyes, is all," I told them. "I'm doing really great cleaning up my room." But even I didn't believe that.

"Okay, *fine*," I said, wiping away the tears so I could see how mad they were at me. "I am s-o-r-r-y, *sorry*! And I won't be like this anymore!"

"Like what, Clementine?" my mom asked. "What are you talking about?"

"Like whatever you don't want," I said. "I won't talk so much and I'll clean up my room for real and I will Think About the Consequences before I do stuff and I won't do stuff anyway and I will never lose my homework because I will never lose anything and I will sit so still you will think 'Hey, is that Clementine or just a statue of Clementine?' and I will never bring another note home that says 'Clementine had a difficult day at school today,' and I will bring hundreds of notes home that say, 'Wow, Clementine certainly pays attention in school!' and the underneath of my bed will look like the underneath of normal people's beds and my hands will always be where they belong and I will take piano lessons again but this time I will sit on the bench the whole time and . . ."

And then I ran out of air. I took a big gulp.

"I won't be like me anymore. And then I'll be the easy one, too, as easy as Celery. So you don't have to get rid of me which I know about because I heard you say 'One's all we need' and then I heard you order a cake that says 'Good-bye and Good Riddance, Clementine!'"

My parents both ran over to me and hugged me at the same time—a hug sandwich. Then they took my hands and brought me out to the dining room.

And there was Margaret and her mother, and

Mitchell with my brother on his shoulders, all looking at me. I scrubbed my face to make sure there weren't any tears left, even though I did *not* care what Mitchell thought because he's *not* my boyfriend.

My brother yelled, "Prize!" and everybody else yelled, "Surprise!" and then they stepped out of the way so I could see the dining-room table.

And on it was a cake, all right. But it didn't say *Good-bye and Good Riddance, Clementine*, it said *Good-bye and Good Riddance!* above a thousand frosting pigeons and then under that it said *Thank You, Clementine—Hero of The Great Pigeon War!*

Oh.

"Well, what about the 'One's all we need' thing?" I asked. "What about that?"

My mom and my dad smiled really, really big then.

"Wait right here, Sport," Dad said. He went into the hall and came back with a big box. "Open it up."

So I did. And do you know what was in there?

A kitten! I am not kidding you.

"There was only one left," Dad said. "And we told them, 'One's all we need.'"

I lifted the kitten out of the box and took him into the bathroom to get him a name. Right away I

found the most exquisite word. I held him up to my cheek and told him his name and he started to purr, which filled up a space in my ears that had been empty since Polka died.

When I came back out, I saw Margaret wanting

to touch my kitten and I saw her tell her hands to be quiet about that because he was mine and he was new.

I wanted to say, *The rule is no touching my kitten because it's the rule.* But I didn't. Instead my mouth opened up and said, "Want to pat Moisturizer, Margaret?" which was a very big surprise, let me tell you.

"We know it's not the same as having Polka Dottie back . . ." my mom started.

"He's different . . ." my dad said.

"I know," I told them. "He's perfect."

Then I looked up and saw that *everything else* was perfect, too: my mother in her overalls, my comedian father, my brother who didn't get stuck with a fruit name, Margaret in her Margaret hat, Mitchell slicing the Clementine-the-Hero cake, my not-from-a-magazine apartment. So

when Margaret's mother came over and said, "Tomorrow after school I'm taking both you girls to my hairdresser to fix up those haircuts," I almost said "No, thanks!" because I didn't want to change a single thing.

But she was smiling at me and that looked perfect, too, so I smiled back and said, "Great!"

And then I passed out the cake and I was extremely polite because I served everyone else a slice first and then at the very end I took one.

Two. Okay, fine.

· · · · · · · ·

ABOUT THE AUTHOR AND ILLUSTRATOR

Sara Pennypacker is also the author of *The Talented Clementine*; *Stuart's Cape* and *Stuart Goes to School*; *Dumbstruck*; and *Pierre in Love*. She was a painter before becoming a writer, and has two absolutely fabulous children who are now grown. Sara lives on Cape Cod in Massachusetts.

Marla Frazee illustrated the second book in this series, *The Talented Clementine*. She is the author and illustrator of many picture books as well, including *Walk On!*, *Santa Claus the World's Number One Toy Expert*, and *Roller Coaster*, and illustrated *The Seven Silly Eaters* and *Everywhere Babies*. Marla works in a small backyard cabin under an avocado tree in Pasadena, California.

Here's a sneak peek of

The Talented Clementine

. . . .

I have noticed that teachers get *exciting* confused with *boring* a lot. But when my teacher said, "Class, we have an exciting project to talk about," I listened anyway.

"Our school is going to raise money for the big spring trip," he said. "The first and second grades are going to hold a bake sale. The fifth and sixth grades are going to have a car wash. And the third and fourth grades are going to . . . put on a talent show!"

All the kids in the room made sounds as if they

thought a talent show was exciting news. Except me, because it was N-O-T, *not*.

But okay, fine, it wasn't boring, either.

Just then, Margaret's teacher came to the door to talk to my teacher, which was good because it gave me an extra minute to think.

"Old people love to pat my little brother's head," I said when my teacher walked back into the room. "How about we set up a booth and charge them a quarter to do it, instead of having a talent show?"

But he ignored me, which is called Getting on with the Day when a teacher does it, and Being Inconsiderate when a kid does it.

"Class," he said, "one of the fourth graders has come up with a name for our show! Talent-Palooza, Night of the Stars!"

It had to be that Margaret.

"First, we'll need a cooperative group to make some posters. . . ." my teacher said.

And that's when the worried feeling—as if somebody were scribbling with a big black crayon—started up in my brains.

My teacher kept on going with the cooperative group list. The scribbling got harder and faster and spread down into my stomach. I knew what this meant.

I raised my hand.

"Yes, Clementine? Would you like to be in the cooperative group for refreshments?"

"No, thank you," I said, extra politely. "What I'd like is to go to Mrs. Rice's office."

"Clementine, you don't need to go see the principal," my teacher said. "You're not in any trouble."

"Well, it's just a matter of time," I told him.

My teacher looked at me as if he suddenly had

no idea how I'd gotten into his classroom. But then he gave a big sigh and said, "All right," so I got up.

As I left, the O'Malley twins gave me the thumbs-up sign, which made me feel like I wasn't alone. But they were wearing their "Thank goodness it's not me" faces, which made me know that I was.

I walked down the hall on worried legs and knocked on the door with worried knuckles.

"Come in," Principal Rice said. When she saw it was me, she held out her hand for the note from my teacher that would tell her what kind of a little chat we should have. We have done this a lot.

But today I just sat on the chair and started right in. "Which are smarter? Chimpanzees or orangutans?"

"That's an interesting question, Clementine," Mrs. Rice said. "Maybe you could ask the science teacher after you've told me what you're doing here."

"Also, I've been wondering what the difference is between *smashed* and *crashed*."

Mrs. Rice handed me her dictionary.

And then suddenly I didn't want to know anymore! That is the miracle about dictionaries!

"Well, how about you put it on the floor so you can rest your feet on it instead of kicking my desk?" Principal Rice suggested. "You seem to have very busy feet today."

So I did, and it felt good. "Thank you," I said.

"I don't have any talents."

"Excuse me?" said Principal Rice.

"I don't have any talents," I said again.

Mrs. Rice looked at me for a long time and then she said, "Oh."

Then I told her I was all done being there and I left.

When I got off the bus, Margaret's brother, Mitchell, was sitting on the front steps of our apartment building.

"What's the matter, Clementine?" he asked me right away—I guess my worried face was still on.

I handed him the stupid flyer my teacher had sent home with us.

"'Talent-Palooza, Night of the Stars! Share your talents Saturday night!'" he read. Then he handed the stupid flyer back to me. "So, what's the problem?"

I leaned over—but not too close in case he thought I was trying to be his girlfriend, which I am not—and whispered the problem to him.

"I can't hear you," he said.

So I whispered it again.

"I still can't hear you," he said.

So I yelled it.

"That's impossible," he said. "Everybody has a talent."

"Not me."

"No singing?"

"No singing."

"No dancing?"

"No dancing."

"No musical instruments?"

"No musical instruments."

Mitchell was quiet for a minute.

"How about hopping?" he asked finally.

"No hopping," I answered.

"Everyone can hop," Mitchell said.

"Not me." Then I proved it to him.

"Wow," said Mitchell. Twice.

I sat down on the step beside him. Except I fell

off, because my body was a little confused from trying to hop. "See?" I said. "I can't even do sitting. It's hopeless."

"Maybe not. Cheer up. Maybe you have a really great talent you just haven't figured out yet."

I gave Mitchell a "See? I'm cheered up already!" smile. But it was just my mouth pretending.

IF YOU ENJOYED THE
CLEMENTINE BOOKS, LOOK FOR

Waylon!
One Awesome Thing

SARA PENNYPACKER

PICTURES BY
Marla Frazee